The Secret of Monks Island

by Griselda Gifford
illustrated by Stewart Lees

Contents

PEARSON
Longman

Text © Griselda Gifford 2003
Series editors: Martin Coles and Christine Hall

PEARSON EDUCATION LIMITED
Edinburgh Gate
Harlow
Essex CM20 2JE
England

www.longman.co.uk

First published 2003
ISBN 0582 79617 2

Illustrated by Stewart Lees

To Jim, with love. And with thanks to Mary Hayes for her help with the
Anglo-Saxons and Vikings.

Printed in Great Britain by Scotprint, Haddington

The publishers' policy is to use paper manufactured from sustainable forests.

1 Monkswell Guest House

"It's so cold!" Alice complained, as we got out of the car in front of Monkswell Guest House. "And windy."

"Bracing," Mum said, with a smile.

"I'm not cold and I like the smell of the sea," I said, partly because Alice was annoying me as usual with her complaining. She's three years older than me and never stops showing off. All right, she's good at ballet and school work, and she's neat, and I suppose pretty if you like looking like a doll ... As for me – I'm tall and thin with big feet and I'm good at swimming – the best in my school. And I'm also very good at imagining things but hopeless at writing them down.

"I can't wait to sketch the house!" Mum said. "The advert said parts of it date from medieval times."

"That means very old, Sammy," Alice explained, maddeningly.

I stared at the house. I looked out over the waves and saw a small rocky island outlined against the sky. I was tired and hungry, but I felt a strange excitement as if our holiday was going to be quite different this year. I shivered – not from cold, but I had one of my weird feelings that sent icy fingers down my spine. I could see danger ahead.

"It's going to be a really good holiday here – swimming, walking, birdwatching," Dad said, as he took the cases out of the car and released Bertie, our mixed-up dog who has Spaniel ears and Dalmatian spots.

Bertie ran straight to the front door and jumped up at the woman who stood there. Our landlady was very tall – not skinny like me but strong-looking like a man. Her fair hair hung in a long plait down her back and her eyes were a brilliant blue.

"Mrs Cuthbertson – I'm so sorry we're late but it's a long drive," Mum said. "This is Sammy and Alice, and my husband, Aidan."

"A good name," Mrs Cuthbertson murmured, strangely, and then we were all inside and being shown our rooms.

"Not even carpet!" Alice said, looking disgustedly at the ancient wooden floor. But I was staring out of the window as the sky and sea became darker.

I heard yowling and barking and opened the door. A cat, blown into a great ball of fur, hissed past and I grabbed Bertie before he made even more of a nuisance of himself.

A boy about my age came out of another bedroom. "Can't you control him?" he said, scornfully. "You'd better tie him up while we have supper," he snapped.

"Who says?" I snapped back, having no intention of obeying him. Bertie hates being tied up.

"*I* say. I'm Eddie Cuthbertson."

I ran ahead of him down the stairs, Bertie following.

"I don't like that boy," Alice whispered as she joined us in the hall.

"Yeah, he's not friendly."

When Mrs Cuthbertson said supper was ready I let Bertie follow me and hide under the table.

A man with a pointy beard joined us and sat between Alice and me.

Mrs Cuthbertson introduced him. "This is Mr Larsen – he's a researcher for television." She began to ladle out thick vegetable soup.

Mr Larsen smiled, "Call me Sven, please. Yes, I'm researching a TV film about the Vikings and the ancient Saxon churches in this area."

Alice looked interested for once. If her future career as a ballerina didn't work out she thought she'd like to act in films. "I got top marks for my Viking project at school," she told him, in her usual show-off way. "They were horribly bloodthirsty, weren't they?"

"Some of the time," he agreed, smiling. "But I suppose as I am of Scandinavian descent, I am related to the Vikings and should defend them!" He turned to Mrs Cuthbertson. "I believe part of this house is built on the foundations of a monastery guest house and chapel?" She nodded and he flashed his very white teeth at her. "And what about the monks' well that gave this house its name?"

"That's completely disappeared. Only part of one wall of the chapel remains. I believe the Vikings burnt it down and killed any monks who hadn't escaped. They did just the same on the island. There are the remains of a Saxon church and the site of the original monastery over there."

Blood red fire at the windows ... I imagined screams and saw cloaked figures running from the house, and again I shivered.

"How do you get to the island?" I asked Mrs Cuthbertson.

"There's a causeway you can walk over at low tide," she said. "Monks Island actually belongs to us. But the church ruins are dangerous and we don't like people disturbing the seabirds. Perhaps Eddie can take you one day. You have to know the times of the tides or you could be stranded when the causeway is covered with water."

* * * * *

After supper Sven left the room and Alice went to watch TV with Mum and Dad. I took Bertie out for his evening walk.

How was I supposed to know that Sven would be coming in from his car at that moment, carrying books in a cardboard box? It wasn't my fault that Bertie leaped up so Sven dropped everything all over the hall. He said some words I'm not allowed to use and both of us, hindered by Bertie, began to pick things up. Some of the

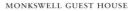

books were leather-bound and looked really old.

"Your stupid dog!" Sven muttered, as I peered under an old wooden seat. I pulled out a book with a battered leather cover and saw the title in gold print:

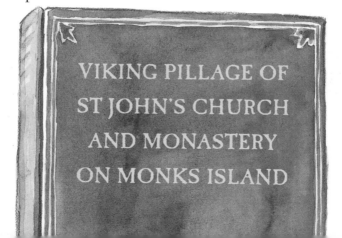

VIKING PILLAGE OF
ST JOHN'S CHURCH
AND MONASTERY
ON MONKS ISLAND

As I picked it up an envelope fluttered out. Bertie seized it and ran upstairs, and I ran after him. Sven was still packing the books back into the box and hadn't noticed.

It was only when I caught Bertie in our room that I realised I was still holding the book. In a cross voice I told Bertie to drop the envelope. A typed letter had fallen out, addressed to Professor Sven Larsen.

I just had time to read the first paragraph:

Dear Dr Larsen,

The artefacts you believe are hidden on the island would interest us a great deal for our overseas clients, who were so pleased with the other valuable goods you discovered. You will be well rewarded for your efforts. Obviously, you must keep your movements secret from any local people because
 ̶ ̶you from taking

At that moment there was a knock on the door. "I dropped an important letter," Sven called.

I put the letter in the damp envelope and, for some reason, I don't really know why, I pushed the book under my bed as he came in. "I'm sorry. I've only just managed to get it back from my dog. I hope he hasn't chewed it."

Sven's pale blue eyes were staring into mine in a weird and menacing way.

I had one of my strange feelings and knew I couldn't trust him.

2 Viking Treasures

I couldn't understand the book. Some of it was in a funny sort of English and the rest was in a foreign language. Then Alice came in. "You're supposed to be going to bed," she said in her bossy way. What are you hiding under your pillow?"

"Don't be so nosy!" I snapped. I didn't dare leave the book while I went to the bathroom, so I sat on my pillow and watched while Alice did her stupid ballet practice.

"I need new ballet shoes," she grumbled as she held on to a chair with one hand, practising her stupid foot positions.

"Mum and Dad have spent loads on your ballet stuff already," I said, while my mind skittered about trying to think how to get the book back to Sven before he noticed it had gone. Then I remembered that Alice was good at

English as well as dancing. "What does 'pillage' mean?"

"'Pillage' … I think it means soldiers or people stealing and ruining things when they invade an enemy country. Why do you want to know?"

Luckily, at that moment Mum came to say it was bedtime. While Alice argued that it was too early, I slipped the book under the bed again.

I couldn't go to sleep for ages because I was worrying about how to get the book back to Sven, but at last I hit on an idea. As I grew sleepy, I imagined myself following Sven to discover what he was really doing at the guest house. I reckoned the letter I'd seen was in code and all to do with drug smuggling. 'Artefacts' was probably a code name for drugs. Someone would land a boat on the island and Sven would sell them the 'artefacts' for millions. I'd somehow foil his plans and everyone would say how brave I was.

Then I was dreaming of misty beaches and running after Sven. Suddenly he loomed over me wearing Viking horns and waving a flaming torch, and I was trying to run away but I couldn't move … I screamed as a wave hit me, and I woke up to feel a wet sponge dripping on my face.

"You woke me up yelling!" Alice said.

I threw the sponge back at her and Mum came in to tell us off, saying it was only five a.m.

Actually, I'd planned to get up early, so I waited a bit longer to give Mum and Alice time to go to sleep again, then I dressed and crept downstairs with the book. Bertie fell on me with joy. I put the book in his basket, under the blanket. To stop him chewing it I took him out of the back door.

He disappeared into the sea mist. I heard a faint woofing in the direction of the beach, so I ran after him over the bumpy dunes.

Only the top of the rocky island showed
through the mist. I followed the sound of Bertie
barking. I could just see him on the sands, tearing
in circles round Sven. "Call him off!" he shouted.
"He's got my papers!"

Now I was nearer
I saw Bertie was
carrying something
in his mouth. The
moment Sven got
near him he
danced away.

"Drop it!" I said
sternly. Bertie just looked
at me and pranced
some more. I found
a dog biscuit in my
pocket and grabbed the
papers when he dropped
them. I noticed there was
a map printed with the words
'Archaeological Survey of Monks Island 2000'.

"Sorry." I handed the papers to Sven.

"I need them for my research," he snapped,
moving away from Bertie. "Keep him off. He
needs training."

"He's only eighteen months old."

I thought I'd play up to his lies. "It's a good morning for getting the spooky feeling of the place for the film people, isn't it?" I said. "I could just see a Viking ship coming out of the mist, couldn't you?"

"I'd hoped to video some footage today but it's too misty so far," he said. "By the way, I seem to have mislaid one of my books. Did the dog take that too?"

"Sorry. I'll go back and search for it," I said meekly.

He followed me back to the house and my plan worked. Bertie went to his basket, scrabbled under the blanket and brought out the book in his mouth. I thought Sven would have a fit. "Put it down! It's very old and valuable!"

Bertie gave a playful growl and Sven backed away, looking scared.

"He won't bite," I said.

"I don't like dogs. I was badly bitten once."

I managed to get the book out of Bertie's mouth and gave it to Sven. "It's only a bit damp. He must have taken it last night. You bad dog!" I felt rather mean, but Bertie wagged his tail.

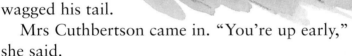

Mrs Cuthbertson came in. "You're up early," she said.

"I was getting the feel of the place," Sven smiled in his smarmy way. "This area is steeped in ancient history, Mrs Cuthbertson."

"Oh, do call me Beba," she said.

"Named after the Anglo-Saxon Queen?" he asked.

"Yes. My father's family comes from this area. Eddie is named after Edwin, a king of Northumbria."

"Well, I hope you won't feel I am a Viking invader to your house!" he joked.

A little grey cat leaped through an open window and sat on the fridge, looking down at Bertie with unfriendly yellow eyes. Mrs Cuthbertson stroked her. "Loki will get used to your dog," she said.

"So you named her Loki, after the Viking god: a mischievous spirit," Sven said.

"Yes, you've certainly done your homework!" said Mrs Cuthbertson. "We found the cat sitting on the beach and she followed us home. You could say she invaded us!"

While we were all having breakfast Sven asked about Monks Island again. "I can go on my own

if Eddie here is too busy to show me." Eddie left
half his cereal and went out.

I saw Dad looking rather horrified. He's strict
about manners. Mrs Cuthbertson just looked sad.
"I'm sorry he's being rude, but it's been difficult
for him since his father's death." She stopped and
looked out of the window a moment, then went
on in a low voice. "My husband died on the
island last spring. He was a wildlife photographer
and worked for the nature conservation people.
We think he was concentrating on photographing
the birds and slipped on a cliff path ..." she tailed
off. Then she grew brisk. "So we prefer to
supervise guests."

Sven put his hand over hers on the table. "I am
so very sad to hear that. Of course the boy's still
upset."

19

Mum and Dad said how sorry they were too and there was a silence.

Then Mrs Cuthbertson said, "You can see why I don't really care to go there at the moment, but it's a lovely little island," she said. "You can see seals and sea otters if you're lucky, and many types of seabirds – kittiwakes, dunlin, oystercatchers, terns, skuas …"

Dad looked excited. "Sounds wonderful! I've brought binoculars and bird identification books with me."

Sven smiled at Mrs Cuthbertson. "By the way, have you had any archaeologists come to dig here?"

Why did he ask when he knew already from that map?

"Yes, here and on the island," she said. "They found some coins and a runic stone … but nothing else."

"Runes," Sven paused. "Now this is all part of my research. Weren't they used by the Vikings for secret charms or curses? I suppose it's in the museum now?"

He was certainly a good liar!

"I bet Sammy doesn't know what an archaeologist is!" Alice said with a smug smile.

It was true, but I wouldn't have admitted it.

"They're experts who dig over ancient places to look for bones, cooking pots, jewels and so on."

"Well, I'd like to go to the island just as soon as Eddie feels like it," Dad said. "But of course, it is a bit misty still. And I've just discovered that my camera battery's gone flat and I forgot to bring a spare. It'll mean going into town."

Alice's face lit up. "I could look for new ballet shoes."

"I believe there's a castle," Mum said eagerly.

I wanted to stay. Sven had left the room, with some story about notes to write up. "Won't Bertie need a walk?" I asked. "I'll stay and give him a really good run on the beach."

There was a lot of fuss about my not going too far away, and Mrs Cuthbertson said she'd ring her ship's bell at lunchtime. Then Dad wanted to wait for the mist to lift and Mum wanted to draw the house, so it was ages before they drove off.

There was no sign of Eddie or Sven, but as Bertie and I came out onto the beach I saw our early footprints had been overlaid with a new set, going towards the causeway. Bertie began to sniff around like a bloodhound and disappeared along the trail into the mist.

I called but he didn't come back, so I ran after him to where the wet sand was covering up the footprints leading to the edge of the causeway, which was now visible like a grey hump above the shallow waves. There was a large notice saying 'PRIVATE'. Bertie was running along it, so I decided to follow him. Perhaps Sven was on the island, collecting a hoard of drugs!

The causeway ended with rocky steps cut into

the cliff. Gulls swooped past with mournful cries as I climbed up the steps into the mist. I had one of my feelings again. I thought I saw Sven as he had looked in my dreams, dark and menacing, coming towards me with a knife in his hand.

I stopped, feeling shaky. Then I told myself it was all in my imagination; I knew I had to be brave and uncover Sven's secrets. But I was only eleven and he was big and strong. He might have a knife or a gun! Or what if he pushed me off the cliff and pretended it was an accident?

I went on, with my heart pounding.

I told myself this was my chance to be brave, to show everyone, especially Alice, that I could catch a dangerous criminal. All the same, I was going to keep out of Sven's sight.

There were two paths at the top of the steps. I could see the vague shapes of the ruins one way, but I heard a faint growling from the other direction. It was too misty to see how close the path was to the edge of the cliff, so I had to walk very carefully.

The faint noises turned into familiar digging sounds and muffled yelps, and I soon came to a pile of rocks and earth. Rabbits had burrowed holes under the rocks and Bertie's long tail stuck out of one of the holes.

I called him and pulled at his sandy rear end. He struggled but backed out with something dangling from his mouth. I managed to take it from him and rubbed the sand off some multicoloured stone beads strung together on a silver wire. There was a medallion hanging from it. I rubbed at it and saw the beautifully decorated metal. It looked old. Could this be a Viking treasure the experts hadn't found?

I scrabbled into the earth Bertie had kicked out and felt a small hard lump, like a big pebble. When I rubbed the earth off I saw it was a big ring.

Bertie had gone back to dig. This time he brought out something rounded, like part of a bowl, which I managed to prise out of his mouth. I rubbed off some of the earth and stared.

I was holding part of a human skull with a hole in it!

3 The Secret Room

I felt a bit sick, thinking of all the films I'd seen about skeletons and unsolved murders. Should I tell the police? I hated holding the skull, so I held Bertie while I pushed it as far back into the hole as I could. I'd decide what to do about it when I got back to the guest house.

Bertie suddenly whined and pulled away, back up the path.

I stuffed the medallion and the ring into my pockets and followed him. The mist was patchy now, and I followed Bertie up the other path towards the ruins. He stopped by a barbed wire fence.

I heard a faint scraping sound coming from somewhere inside the crumbling walls. I guessed at once it was Sven up to no good, so I tugged at Bertie's collar, dragging him away to hide behind some bushes.

I waited, wondering what to do. Mrs Cuthbertson would soon be ringing the bell for lunch. I wanted to catch Sven red-handed and yet I had to get back.

Bertie looked up, waving his tail. I peered through a gap in the bushes and saw Sven climbing over the wire with a spade in his hand.

He threw it into the bushes, just missing Bertie and me, and slithered off down the cliff path to the steps. He was carrying a backpack, which was probably stuffed with drugs.

I held on tight to Bertie's collar and waited so Sven could get across the causeway. If he suspected I was following him I'd never find out anything. Now, in among the calling of the seabirds, I heard the faint sound of a bell.

By the time Bertie and I got down the cliff steps, the sun had burst through the mist and I could see the causeway was empty. But it was also under water. I started walking along it, but the water was quite deep and it pulled at my legs. I knew I'd never keep my feet on the rough stones and decided it would be much easier to swim. It looked only about a hundred and fifty metres or so, and I'd swum much more than that in the pool at home. The water was cold and it took my breath away for a moment.

It wasn't easy swimming in my jeans and
trainers, and half-way across I slowed down. Then
I saw Bertie's head bobbing in the wavelets,
swimming beside me, and this gave me new energy.

When at last I sloshed up the sands I saw
Eddie, grinning like mad. "Fancy swimming with
your clothes on! My mother's worried about you.
Sven came in from a walk, but he said he hadn't
seen you." He didn't sound quite as unfriendly as
when we arrived, even though he knew I'd been to
their private island.

"I didn't mean to worry your mum," I said.
"Bertie ran down the causeway after Sven. I went
after him and found Sven in the ruined church. I
think he's up to something. And Bertie dug up
some sort of old jewels and ..." I couldn't say
any more because Mrs Cuthbertson
was walking

towards us, looking both cross and worried.

"You're wet! Did you fall in?" she asked. "Where did you go?"

"She was playing some game with her dog and fell in," Eddie said quickly.

I didn't know why he'd suddenly decided to help me, but I was grateful. Mrs Cuthbertson bustled me inside to change before lunch. I transferred the jewels to my dry clothes.

Sven wasn't at lunch and I was glad I didn't have to face him. Eddie didn't talk while he was eating, but afterwards he stopped me in the hall.

"If you'll show me the jewels you found," he whispered, "I'll show you the ruin of the chapel behind the house. And we can talk about Sven. I'm suspicious of him, too."

"I thought you hated us all," I said.

"I just wish we didn't need to have guests in the house," he answered as we walked outside and round the back of the house, followed by Bertie. "But we need the money to go on living here. And the roof needs mending." He sighed. "I don't know why I'm telling you all this. Anyway, these walls are the remains of a small chapel attached to the monks' guest house." He waved his arm at the ancient, moss-covered stones. "And there was another place they used under the old guest house."

He led me to some steps, down into a vaulted cellar full of boxes and junk. "This is the only bit left of their guest house."

He brought out a torch and then pulled aside two heavy boxes. I saw a jagged opening in the ancient brickwork. Darkness lay behind.

"I can't think why nobody's ever found this before," he said.

"I discovered it almost by accident. I'd read a story about walls sounding hollow when there was a secret room, so I tapped round, moving things, and this bit sounded different. Some of the bricks were crumbling, but it took ages to make the hole. I didn't tell Mum because I thought I'd just keep it as a secret den to get away when our house is full of guests." He shone the torch and I could see the bare stone walls of a small room. Bertie jumped through the hole and went sniffing round.

We scrambled inside. Eddie lit candles he'd put in jam jars and I saw the damp stone-flagged floor and a cobwebbed cross on the wall. There was a big wooden chair and a table with a carved box on it. I shivered with the chill and the smell of damp and decay. "Who'd want to stay in here?" I asked.

"Maybe it was a hermit: a monk who lived alone," he suggested.

Then I saw something like a coffin in a dark corner. "Is there someone buried in there?" I asked, trying to stop my voice quivering.

"Don't be a twit!" he said. "Can't you see it's a sort of bed? Now it's your turn, Sam. Show me what you found."

I brought out the ring and the medallion on its string of carved stone beads. I'd washed them while I was changing and now the medallion shone silver in the candlelight. It was beautifully engraved with a design of leaves and flowers. The stones in the necklace part were all different colours, and I wondered if they were valuable.

"That's interesting," he said, taking it from me and examining it closely.

Then I showed him the ring. Now it was clean it shone gold and was set with a circle of red stones. Perhaps they were rubies. Eddie shone the torch close up to it and we could see there was a kind of writing inside or a design, like little stick-marks.

"I think this might be Viking jewellery that the archaeologists didn't find," he said. "There was this same funny stick-writing on the stone they found. They're called runes."

"I know. Sven told us. The Vikings sometimes used runes for secret spells or curses." When he gave the ring back to me I had a feeling that the ring held a magic power, but I knew Eddie would laugh at me if I said anything.

I thought I'd better tell him about Bertie's other find. "I found a bit of a skull as well, in the same place. With a hole in it. But I put it back." Even the thought of it made me cold.

"Cool! It sounds like you found a Viking grave." He sounded excited. "The archaeologists must have missed it when they were on the island. In one of Dad's books I read that sometimes they killed a slave girl and threw her into the grave so the Viking lord would have company."

I had a sudden feeling and shuddered so

strongly that I felt sick. I could see a girl
screaming, her hands and feet bound, and a
Viking who looked like Sven slashing at her head
with his sword! "No!" I whispered.

Eddie was clutching my arm. "What's the
matter?"

But I knew if I told him he'd think I was mad.
"I feel a bit sort of buried in here," I said.

He was still looking at the medallion, swinging
it round so it caught the light. "It's a good thing
Sven didn't find these treasures. But what was he
looking for in the church?"

"I think he's hiding drugs there," I said. "He dropped a letter. It said he'd be well rewarded for finding artefacts for clients abroad. I think it was some sort of code about drugs. They'll bring the drugs by boat from …" I stopped as I tried to think what country was across the sea from this coast, but I'm not very good at geography.

Eddie was laughing at me. "From Scandinavia? But I don't think it's drugs; you've watched too much TV! It sounds as though the letter's from a dealer in ancient treasures, who could sell them abroad to collectors. It looks like Sven's onto something. But you have to report it if you find ancient treasures. It's called Treasure Trove. You can't just take them. And sometimes people get rewards. Anyway, those treasures belong here, not thousands of miles away in a private collection. Where exactly did you find the medallion and the ring?"

"Near a path to the right of the church. But can't we keep it quiet for a bit? We'll never catch Sven red-handed if people start coming to dig on the island." I paused. "I suppose you could be right about Sven looking for treasures. He did have old books and one was about Monks Island and the Viking pillages in this area."

"Sounds very suspicious," Eddie said. "But we

can't prove anything yet. We'll have to follow
him. I found a book myself, hidden in this old
box. I put it back because it's falling apart." He
took a heavy book out of the carved box. Part of
the leather cover was eaten away
by mould. Carefully, he opened
it and shone the torch on
the first page.

We looked at the
strange words,
wreathed in
beautiful
designs of
flowers
and animals.

"Impressive,
isn't it?" he said.
"I suppose it's in
Latin. And this was
loose inside." Very
carefully, he lifted out a page. "It looks as if it's
been written in a hurry, but not in Latin. There
aren't any pictures, but there's a sort of map at the
bottom. I've had a go at making out the words
and I've written them down. I was going to look
in one of Dad's old books to translate them." He
brought an old exercise book out of the box.

He'd written carefully: 'On mynster waes sum goldhord and seolfre'. "I think I've got the letters right," he said. "Then if you look at the original writing there's a mouldy bit which blotted the words so all I got then was: 'wael-fyr … Dene …' I suppose it's the Anglo-Saxon language the monks spoke when they didn't use Latin. Dad told me about it."

"I bet Alice knows," I said. I peered hard at the letters. "Probably the word 'on' might be the same as it is now. And do you think 'goldhord' might be something like a hoard of gold?"

"I thought that," Eddie said quickly. "And I suppose 'mynster' could be a monastery unless it's 'monster'," he added. "And if you say 'seolfre' quickly it sounds a bit like silver."

I was looking at the drawing below the message. There was a picture of a building with an archway and a cross on top. There seemed to be three floors with an arrow pointing downwards. Then there were three boxes, one with a skull on top. The building was on a hump surrounded by wiggly lines, marked 'see'. After the wiggles were another two buildings, one small with a cross on top.

"I think it's a map," I said. "The humpy bit could be Monks Island with the church and monastery."

"I thought that too," he said quickly. (I bet he hadn't!) "And the 'see' could be 'look at this' or their way of writing 'sea'. And here's a building with another cross on top. I bet that's here, the old guest house and chapel. I think it's a map and a message, left when the monks were running away from the Vikings. Perhaps the last monk in the monastery hid the treasure and left this map for the hermit to look after."

"And then other monks could come back and find the treasure. But nobody came back." I had another feeling, this time of aching loneliness and fear and I wanted to cry. A horrible thought struck me. "I wonder when the entrance was bricked in?"

We were both silent.

Then Eddie said, "Perhaps the Vikings found the treasure anyway."

I swallowed but my voice sounded odd. "Or a survivor came back for it. So there might be nothing to find." I felt really disappointed at the thought. Bertie nudged my foot with something hard. "Shine your torch down," I told Eddie. "It's a big bone!"

"Too big for an animal," he said. "Sort of long, like a leg bone."

We both stared at the bed in the dark corner. Eddie shone his torch. Something white and round gleamed in the darkness.

"It's a skull!" we said at the same time.

"The hermit must have died here!" Eddie said.

4 Treasure Map

"Better leave the book and the monk's map here," Eddie said. "Safer, till we've decided whether to tell anyone."

I couldn't wait to get out, but then I remembered something.

"Let's copy the map," I said. "Then we can find the treasure before Sven does."

Eddie had a pencil in his pocket and he scrawled a copy of the map under his translation of the words. Then I pulled at Bertie's collar because he wanted to look at the remains of the hermit.

When we were back in the cellar, Eddie pushed the boxes back into place across the hole. "One of us will have to watch Sven all the time," he said, as we went out into the fresh air.

"I'm going to hide these jewels for now," I said.

"Okay. But don't forget and take them home, will you?"

"Of course not," I snapped. Then I saw he was grinning.

I hid the jewels in our bedroom, in my wash bag, and I put it on the shelf above my bed.

The others had just got back from the town. Mum was particularly cross to hear I'd been late for lunch and got wet through. Dad gave me one of his teacher-type lectures on being responsible and Alice waved her new ballet shoes and leotard at me. "You should've come. We had a brilliant pizza."

"The castle was very interesting," Dad said to Mrs Cuthbertson. "And the museum. We saw the runic stone that was found on the island, and the Viking coins. Fascinating."

Eddie and I were trying not to look at each other.

"With a name like Aidan you should be interested," Mrs Cuthbertson said. "He was the great saint of Lindisfarne island, just along the coast from here."

Dad nodded. "I know. My father taught history and he was particularly interested in that period, hence my name."

"Did the monks have a special language?" I asked, trying to sound casual. "Not just Latin?"

Dad nodded. "Anglo-Saxon. Some words you might recognise because they're a bit like ours. And a lot of our language comes from that time."

I could see he was going to give a short lesson, so I asked quickly, "For instance, what was Anglo-Saxon for 'sea'?"

"'S-e-e', I think," he said, spelling it out. "And they called the Vikings the 'Dene'."

"That meant Dane," Alice chimed in. "You could have asked me. I know all that."

But she didn't know what Eddie had found.

* * * * *

It was a golden afternoon; the sea was blue-green and so calm that only tiny wavelets rippled over the sand. Mum brought out her easel and stool and began painting the view of Monks Island. Dad suggested a game of rounders, and to my surprise Eddie joined in. He was nearly as good as me. Alice didn't try because she thinks rounders is babyish. Bertie was rather too helpful, fetching the ball and not returning it, so he had to be tied to Mum's stool and she complained that he jogged her.

Then we all felt too hot to go on and lay on the beach, panting. Dad looked at the island through his binoculars. "Look at all those seabirds! It'll be great to go there."

"I really will take you tomorrow," Eddie promised. I knew he was wondering how we could get there first and look for the treasure.

"When will the water go back from the causeway?" I asked him.

"Low tide is about every twelve and a half hours. This morning the tide was probably at its lowest at about 11.30 – but you can still get across for an hour each side of low tide."

So if Eddie and I or Sven wanted to go to the island again tonight, we'd have to wait until after eleven, or swim!

"Meet you outside after supper," Eddie whispered to me as we walked back with the others.

Alice caught up with us. "Making a date, are you?" She must have heard him. "Little sister Sam is far too young!"

Eddie went bright red, but I thought it was a good ploy. "Too young, am I?" I snapped and I linked my arm in his, trying to look all lovey-dovey.

"What was all that about?" he asked, when we finally escaped from my family. "You keen on me or what?"

"Don't be daft!" I linked arms with him again and marched him round to the back of the house into the ruined chapel. "Alice is so nosy. I don't want her to know about the treasure. Have you got the map? We ought to get there before Sven."

He looked relieved that I'd not fallen for him! "Just what I thought." He unfolded the paper. "It looks as if the treasure's underneath the church. But I'm sure that the archaeologists and local history people went all over the church. Why didn't they find it?"

"Perhaps it's gone." I was puzzling about the arrow on the map which pointed down to boxes and the skull. "Are there tombs under the church?"

"I don't know ..." he began, but he was interrupted by a cheerful shout.

"Hi, you two!" Sven's room was at the back and he was leaning out of the window. "What are you up to?"

Luckily, at that moment Mrs Cuthbertson rang her ship's bell for supper.

"Do you think he saw the map?" I asked.

"Hope not," Eddie said.

* * * * *

At supper Sven went on about the churches again, and then listened carefully to Dad's description of the castle and museum. He said that would be his next visit, after seeing the island. He was such a good liar!

"How about joining us tomorrow when Eddie shows us the island?" Dad suggested.

Sven flashed him a smile. "That's an excellent idea! My producer is especially keen we feature the island so I'll take my camcorder."

Eddie kicked me under the table, a bit harder than necessary.

"Perhaps you'd like to see the old part of the house?" Mrs Cuthbertson asked Sven and Dad after supper, when Alice and Mum had gone upstairs to put cream on their sunburn. Dad smiled enthusiastically and Sven looked like Bertie with a bone.

"I'll take them, Mum," said Eddie.

She laughed. "Anything to get out of the washing-up!"

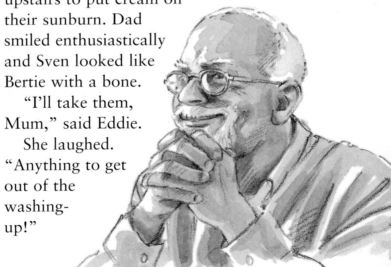

I hovered about outside, throwing a ball for Bertie. We still had to make a plan. When they came back Sven was carrying his camcorder and looking really pleased. "Excellent! We'll certainly film down there. I'd like to go back alone and drink in the atmosphere. Could I move some of the boxes to get the texture of the old bricks?"

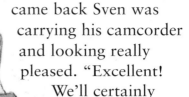

Eddie and I looked at each other in horror.

"Of course you can," Mrs Cuthbertson said. "We should clear it up sometime, anyway. It was full of junk when we arrived and somehow ..." she sighed, "I haven't had the heart to tidy it up."

"I'm going to tell my producer what a wonderful place this is for our film," Sven said. "I should be able to get you a good fee for using your house and the island for filming, and perhaps you might do a short interview yourself, Beba? You'd be a natural on TV." He gave Mrs Cuthbertson one of his flashing smiles and she agreed, rather too eagerly.

Alice was safely practising her dancing and our parents were having coffee and planning outings, so Eddie and I walked to the beach with Bertie. "I hate Sven sucking up to my mother like that," he said. "And what a liar he is!"

I stopped on top of a dune, looking at Monks Island. "I've been thinking – I bet he'll go to the island tonight, at low tide. We ought to get there before him."

Eddie chucked a piece of driftwood for Bertie to fetch. "Of course we must go. But it all depends if everyone's asleep early,

otherwise it'll be difficult to slip out of the house."

"We'll have to take Bertie to stop him whining when he sees us go."

I could just see the jagged top of the ruined church on Monks Island and as I wondered what secrets it held, I had another feeling, even stronger than before. I was underground, running with hooded figures down a long tunnel whose dripping walls seemed to close in on either side so I could hardly breathe. Shouts followed us and death was at our heels ...

5 Following Sven

My legs felt like jelly as we walked back and I was so scared I wanted to warn Eddie. I'd never had such a strong feeling before and I wondered if I was going mad.

When we got back to the house, Alice, wearing her new leotard and shoes, was giving a dancing display in the hall. Mum was smiling as Sven videoed it. "Your sister's going to be a real ballerina!" he said. "I just thought it would be helpful for her to see herself on screen. I might take it back to show the studio for their new project on dancing schools."

"Yuk!" I whispered to Eddie. I wondered why Sven bothered to make up such elaborate lies. Maybe once you started lying you couldn't stop.

"Isn't it kind of Sven?" Mum said.

"Where's Dad?" I asked.

"He's looking at photographs taken by Eddie's father."

I followed Eddie to a study, where the walls were crowded with fantastic photographs of birds, seals, otters and the wild coastal landscape.

Mrs Cuthbertson showed us photographs of the archaeological dig. One was inside the ruined chapel, with people crouched by trenches, examining the earth. The other was taken on the island, near the church, but a little distance from the rocky outcrop where I'd found the Viking jewellery.

"It wasn't easy for the archaeologists on the island because of all the rocks," she said.

I nudged Eddie and then we heard Bertie howl, so we ran out of the room. Alice was sitting on the floor, almost in tears. "That horrible dog knocked me over!" she shouted. Loki was chasing Bertie up the stairs!

Mum was trying not to laugh. "I think he was trying to eat Loki's food!"

Bertie was on my bed, burrowing into my pillow with Loki hissing underneath. I shooed her outside and Bertie jumped off the bed, holding my wash bag. I pulled at it, but he held on and it ripped apart. The jewels clattered to the floor. I grabbed the ring, but Bertie seized the medallion, ready for a game.

Alice came in. "What's he got hold of?" she asked.

"Just something off the beach." I found a mint for him. Bertie dropped the medallion but Alice swooped on it. "It's pretty. Where did you find it?" she asked.

"Give it back!" I shouted, but Alice danced out of reach.

She was laughing at me, but when I shouted louder she let go of the medallion. "Have it back then, baby! It's pretty ancient, anyway!"

I thrust it into my pocket with the ring. At least she hadn't seen that.

Mum came in looking cross and asking what all the noise was about. Alice scowled at me, but at least she didn't say anything about the medallion. "It was a childish game of Sam's," she said nastily.

Sometimes I wish I didn't have a sister.

I decided it would be safer to keep the jewels with me in my pockets all the time.

Mrs Cuthbertson gave us tea and homemade biscuits before bedtime. Loki was perched on the dresser, looking down at Bertie, who crouched low, fearing another attack.

"She's rather a strange cat," Mrs Cuthbertson said. "She goes on walks with us, like a dog. Or she stays out all night and we find a dead rat on the doorstep, as a present!"

I shivered. Didn't Mrs Cuthbertson say the cat was named after a mischievous Viking God? I had another feeling. Loki was leaving the house at night, a little grey shadow that turned into a fearsome spirit, part human, part cat, with huge golden eyes and long, long claws …

55

"Are you all right, Sam?" Dad asked.

"I'm fine," I muttered.

"You'd better be," he said. "We're going swimming tomorrow."

"I hate swimming," Alice said sulkily.

"So do I," Sven said. "When I was little, I fell into a pool and nearly drowned and it put me off. Now, Alice, what about this video?"

Eddie and I slipped out of the room to talk. "I'll meet you on the beach at about eleven," he said. "That's if everyone's gone to bed by then. Let's hope we can get there before Sven."

Alice was pleased with the video and came to bed in a much better mood. "Why don't you tell me where you found that medallion thing?" she asked. "Mrs Cuthbertson ought to know if it's valuable."

I decided I had to lie. We didn't want anyone interfering until we'd found the treasures. I crossed my fingers. "Well, actually it's just a copy of a Viking ornament Eddie gave me. I think he fancies me."

She giggled irritatingly. "You're getting big-headed, baby sister!"

I was tired and had to force myself to stay awake, shining my small torch at my watch. Luckily, all the fresh air had made our parents

tired too, and I heard them saying goodnight to
Mrs Cuthbertson as they came upstairs just after
ten. Alice was already asleep. I waited half an
hour and dressed as quietly as I could, creeping
out of the bedroom, scared I might meet Sven.

The stairs creaked and the kitchen door
groaned when I opened it. Bertie leaped out of his
basket, wagging his tail.

Moonlight shone on the dunes and I saw a
small figure ahead, a black shape that must be
Eddie, followed by a small shadowy cat. I ran to
join him. "We'd better hurry to get ahead of
Sven," I began.

"Too late," Eddie said. A dark figure with a torch was coming out of the house. If we weren't careful, Sven would see us!

We hid behind a dune and I held Bertie tight as Sven passed close by, heading for the causeway.

"It would be just our luck if he goes straight to the church," Eddie whispered.

"Unless he's looked there already and not found anything."

Sven's dark shape reached the island and merged into the blackness.

"Come on, Eddie."

"Supposing he sees us?"

"He won't if we're careful," I said. We have to catch him in the act, if he's digging up anything."

I kept Bertie on the lead. At first he kept turning round to see Loki, sitting on the dune, waiting for us to return. Or was she weaving a magic Viking spell?

It seemed unreal, walking on top of the shining, silver sea. I imagined the dark shape of a Viking ghost ship sailing in towards the island. Then I realised it was just the tip of a rock with the moonlight glinting on the white foam.

"Look!" Eddie hissed behind me. I saw a faint light returning down the steps to the causeway. "He's coming back already! He'll see us if we run, then he'll make off with the treasures!"

We were more than half-way over the causeway and there was nowhere to hide. I looked round wildly. Although it was low tide, the sea near the island would be deep enough to cover us. "Jump in!" I hissed.

Bertie obeyed, pulling me in with a splash and the cold water woke me up. Eddie followed. "Can you keep the dog quiet?" he whispered.

Bertie was making his usual puffing noise as he paddled happily round us. I clutched him close to me, hoping he wouldn't make a sound. My head was just above the water, with my feet on the bottom.

"He's got something on his back!" Eddie whispered.

I saw the handle of a spade jutting out of the rucksack, and then he was so near that I hissed, "Go under now!" As I held my breath I tried to pull Bertie down with me but he bobbed up like a cork. Would Sven see him?

6 Alice in Trouble

When I came up for air, Sven was well past us, hurrying towards the shore.

"Now's our chance to look at the church," I said.

"Don't be stupid!" Eddie whispered. "We have to see what he's found."

"I'm not stupid!" I snapped at him. "But we're missing a chance."

As soon as the light of Sven's torch faded, I followed Eddie up onto the causeway again, feeling cross. After all, I was trying to help the Cuthbertson family, wasn't I?

We sloshed back feeling cold and uncomfortable in our wet clothes. Bertie stopped dead when Loki padded up the beach, hissing at him.

Eddie picked her up and we persuaded Bertie to come with us.

When we were in the kitchen, Eddie whispered,

"The spade proves Sven was digging, doesn't it?"

I gave Bertie a biscuit to keep him quiet. "Yes, but did he find anything? After all, he hasn't got our map."

Eddie rubbed his wet hair with a towel. "Unless he's found out from somewhere else. I reckon if he has anything in that rucksack, he could be planning to drive off early in the morning. If he's here at breakfast, then he's found nothing."

I looked at my soggy legs. "That was my last pair of clean jeans. What shall I do?"

Mrs Cuthbertson didn't have a tumble-dryer but she'd hung my other jeans on an old-fashioned clothes airer in the kitchen. We crept round the kitchen, letting down the washing pulley. A pair of my jeans and a T-shirt were nearly dry, so I changed behind the big fridge. I just remembered in time to take the medallion and ring out of the pockets before I put my wet things on the drier next to Eddie's.

I fell into bed and slept late. When I went to breakfast, Sven was still there tucking into eggs and bacon as if nothing had happened in the night. Eddie looked up and shrugged his shoulders when he saw me. I felt excited. There was still a chance we could find the treasure first.

* * * * *

"It's a lovely day," Mum said at breakfast in the kitchen. "I thought we'd swim first and then see the island. You said we could get across in the late morning, didn't you, Beba?"

Mrs Cuthbertson nodded and then Mum noticed water was dripping on her head from the clothes dryer.

"I'm sorry," said Mrs Cuthbertson. "I think Eddie's hung extra washing up without putting it in the spin-dryer."

"Sorry, Mum. I sort of got my jeans splashed by a wave," Eddie said.

Then, luckily, Loki slid into the room and Bertie shot out of the open kitchen door so we both ran after him. We found Bertie in the parking space at the side of the house under our old car, which was next to Sven's brand new car.

"Let's have a look," Eddie said, and we peered in through the boot window. I could just make out the rucksack and a spade. "That rucksack looks empty," I said.

"Yeah," he agreed. "But we've got to watch him all the time. I'll stay with him this morning, whether he wants me to or not."

"Then we've got to get to the church and see for ourselves," I said.

Dad was in one of his energetic moods and Alice grumbled as he led us down the sands to where low cliffs reared up above some rocks. He got excited about some black and white birds, which he said were oystercatchers.

It was hot and Mum plonked herself down in the shadow of a rock with her sketchbook. "I'll swim in a minute," she said. "So will I," Alice said, wandering under the cliffs where pretty clumps of thrift and sea pinks grew on ledges.

"We won't let you off!" Dad shouted, as he and I raced into the sea after Bertie.

I floated on my back, puzzling what we could do about Sven and whether he had found anything. Perhaps we should be searching his room. Should we tell Mrs Cuthbertson about him? But he'd deny it and then we'd never catch him – or find the treasures ourselves. We just had to get to the island again.

Suddenly I heard a shout from the shore. Mum was waving at us.

We swam back. "Alice was looking for flowers and now she's stuck!" Mum said. "I tried to climb after her but I kept slipping back."

I ran to the cliff. Alice was on a ledge with her arms outspread, her face pressed against sheer rock. "I'm dizzy. I'm going to fall!" she shouted.

7 Sam to the Rescue

Mum and Dad both called out telling me to stop, but I had to get my stupid sister down the cliff. She'd gone up a very steep rocky path to the right of the ledge and there was a missing bit where a foothold had crumbled away. Bertie was already trying to scramble up on the left side. This way was steep but had plenty of footholds, and there was a sturdy little bush quite near Alice's ledge.

I called out to Alice that I was coming up. As I climbed, my bare knees hurt almost as much as my bare feet. I'd often dreamed of rescuing someone from a burning house or the sea, but I hadn't imagined a cliff rescue.

I reached the bush and held onto it with one hand. "It's easy, this side," I called to Alice, who was still clinging to the rock face. She turned her head and opened her eyes. I stretched out my hand.

"Come on. I'll
get you down."
"I can't move!" she said hoarsely.
Alice's ledge was at least half a metre
wide, covered in grass and pink flowers.
"You can easily move along a bit," I said.
"Then take your left hand off and hold mine. I'll
go down first and show you the footholds."
"My legs won't work," Alice sobbed.
I'd have to make her mad at me. "Scaredy-cat!"
I shouted. "How'd you like Sven to hear what a
coward you are?"
"Shut up!" she cried, but she moved sideways
and at last she took her left hand off. I grabbed it,
then moved down, finding handholds.

Gradually I got her down, sometimes by actually placing her feet on tiny ledges. We were still about three metres from the ground when she slipped, pushing me down with her. We both slid to the bottom and landed on the pebbly sand with a great thump. Alice lay still, her head near a low rock.

We all bent over her and she slowly looked up, saying her head and her ankle hurt. Dad felt her ankle carefully. "I think it's just a sprain," he decided. "But you were knocked out for a moment, so I need to get you checked at the hospital."

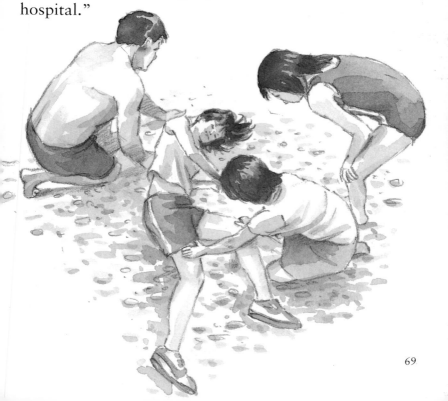

Alice put her arms round Mum and Dad's shoulders and hobbled back between them. I noticed as we passed that the causeway was nearly free of water, but it didn't look as if we'd go there today.

When we got back Dad said he'd drive Alice to the hospital and Mum said she'd go too, in case Alice was kept in. "I hope you don't mind staying here, Sam?" Mum asked. "There just isn't room in the car with Alice stretched out in the back. You did very well, getting her down the cliff."

"I'll look after Bertie," I said, and they drove off.

I was in the kitchen, giving Bertie his food, when Sven strode into the house with Eddie.

"Marvellous day for taking pictures," he said, putting down his camcorder and camera. "I was down in the cellar here again when Eddie came to say he thought he'd seen a seal so I went out with him."

"Oh, I am sorry," he said, when he heard about Alice. "I'll bring her back a present. I'm going off for a day or two. My producer contacted me this morning and he wants me to research some ancient sites further along the coast. But I'll be back very soon." He went upstairs to pack.

"I'm not sure if I interrupted him soon enough in the cellar," Eddie said, when we were on our own. "Mum got me hanging out the washing and Sven just slunk off. I ran to the cellar as quickly as I could and made up some story about a seal. But I've not had time to check down there. Then when we were out, he said he had a message on his mobile and rang the so-called 'producer' back. He only said 'yes' twice and 'speak to you soon'."

"Supposing he has found something and he doesn't come back," I said.

"We can still go to the church ourselves," Eddie reminded me.

When he went, Sven actually kissed Mrs Cuthbertson goodbye! "Or should it be *au revoir?*" he added.

Dad called soon after lunch. "The hospital wants Alice to stay the night because of the bump on her head, but her ankle's only sprained. It's a long way back so we thought we'd stay at a local bed and breakfast. Will you be all right?"

"Of course." I was sorry for Alice but I couldn't help thinking it would be easier for us to get away to the island.

"Come on, Sam," Eddie said when I'd rung off. "Let's go and check the cellar."

I didn't want to go because of the hermit's remains, but I forced myself to follow him.

At once we knew something was wrong. "The boxes in front of the wall aren't how I left them," Eddie said.

We pulled them out and Eddie shone his torch round the cell. The lid was off the carved box and the monks' ancient book had gone!

8 Danger on the Island

We stared at each other in horror.

"Perhaps that book's so valuable it's all Sven wants?" Eddie suggested. "He doesn't know we've found it already."

"But he's clever – he will have seen the map and directions to the treasure," I said. "I think he'll go back there."

"Unless he worked it out earlier somehow and found the treasure himself."

"I still think we've got to follow the map ourselves, even if he's already found the treasure. Otherwise we'll never know. He's not likely to come back. That was all lies," I said.

"I was just going to say that." Eddie sounded a bit annoyed. "We'll go tonight."

* * * * *

Eddie and I took Bertie out on the beach before

supper, just for something to do. Clouds covered the sun and the beach was empty of holidaymakers. The causeway was still under the waves. Suddenly I saw a glint of brightness on the bonnet of a car much further along the shore. "Look!" I said, pointing. "That bright blue – that's the colour of Sven's car!"

We put Bertie on the lead and crept through the dunes, hiding in the stiff grasses. Sven's metallic blue car was parked at the end of a rough track that led to the dunes. I could just see him, slumped in the front seat. "He looks dead!" I whispered.

"Don't be an idiot! He's probably just waiting for low tide," Eddie said. "We'll have to get there before him, tonight." He looked excited. "The water should be nearly off the causeway by about half-past twelve. I'll wake you in time."

It was odd without Alice in the next bed. I didn't undress and tried to read a book to keep myself awake, but it felt a long time until Eddie shone his torch at my face. "Bring your backpack, in case we find anything," he said.

We crept downstairs and out of the house, with Bertie following. He skittered to one side as Loki slid like a little shadow out of the tough dune grass.

The weather had changed and racing clouds covered the moon. I shivered as I saw Monks Island, a dark outline against the dark sky.

As we approached the causeway I had a feeling:
I could see the dark, hooded forms of the monks
as they jostled and ran along the causeway.
Shouts followed them from Vikings waving
burning sticks. For a moment I was one of the
monks and I felt like a hunted animal. Then it
all vanished but it left me with a terrible feeling
of doom.

Bertie bounded onto the causeway. "We're a bit
late," Eddie said. "We'll have to hurry." He
charged after Bertie, splashing through a thin
layer of water. I followed.

Bertie growled softly as we walked up the rocky steps from the causeway, but I couldn't see anything. My heart thudded as we went up the path to the ruined church. I helped Eddie through the barbed wire and Bertie flattened himself underneath, then, before we could stop him, he ran through the church doorway.

"What if Sven's already there and he hurts Bertie!" I whispered, rushing after him, Eddie following. The thin beam of my torch showed that only part of the walls remained and the wind howled eerily round the broken arches and pillars.

"I don't think he's got here yet," I said. "Let's see the map."

The paper flapped in the wind as we held the map between us. "We've got to find the stairs down," Eddie said. "I once came in here with my dad but he said it was too dangerous to explore it properly."

Bertie went round the ruins with us, and now we could see where someone had dug up part of the stone floor. "I bet that was Sven!" I said.

We found an ancient door in one corner, opened it and released a shower of stones. The door led outside. Beyond, I could just see the waves, creamy topped as they broke the darkness.

"No steps here," Eddie said.

I shone the torch to a far corner of the ruins where a roof beam had knocked down a stone pillar. Then I saw footprints in the dust, going into the corner, under the beam.

"Look!" I shone my torch. "A man's footprints!"

"He must be in there," Eddie whispered.

"Let's see." I sounded braver than I felt.

"Don't shift anything. The stones aren't safe," he warned.

We crawled under the beam and found the remains of a wooden door, which gave way when we pushed it.

Stone steps led down into pitch darkness. Bertie pushed ahead of us.

There was a woofing and scrabbling sound as we hurried down, shining our torches, praying that Sven wasn't there already. But the room was empty, except for Bertie, scratching at the floor which was smothered with thick dirt and dust. Some of the floorboards had been prised up. I shone my torch on more footprints. "He's certainly been in here. But the map shows a room under this one, doesn't it?"

We searched round and even looked where Sven had prised up the floorboards. But there was only a dark space, filled with dirt and rubble. "Maybe we've got it wrong and there isn't another room," Eddie said.

Bertie thought it was all a great game and kept scratching the floor, throwing up heaps of dust into our faces.

"Perhaps we'd better give up," Eddie said. "Or the causeway will be covered over."

"That's enough, Bertie!" I sneezed and went to put him on the lead, but I stumbled over something hard. I shone the torch. There was an iron ring.

We pulled at the ring but couldn't move it. The edges were packed with dirt and dust. "At least Sven hasn't found this," Eddie said.

"I've got a penknife in my backpack," I said, slipping it off and fishing around in the muddle of odds and ends. I dug round the edge of the trapdoor with the blade, loosening all the dirt. It was hard work and I was glad to let Eddie have a go when I was half-way round.

"Come on – let's try now!" Eddie said.

We linked hands, heaving at the loop. Slowly the trapdoor creaked open. We shone our torches on more stone steps and more darkness beyond. Musty, age-old air wafted out. I had another feeling, of being buried alive in this place. I even felt I couldn't breathe! I told myself to take no notice; I wanted to help the Cuthbertsons and show Alice how brave I was, didn't I? So I followed Eddie and Bertie down the steps.

We shone our torches round this lower vaulted crypt. This time there were no footprints. Nobody had been here for centuries.

"Aren't those tombs?" I said in a shaky voice. They were made of stone, piled one on top of the other.

"I suppose they buried the monks here," Eddie said hoarsely. "Looks as if the lid of the top one is half-open. They might have something hidden inside."

"Or we might just find a skeleton ..." and I

shivered. I felt sick but I didn't want Eddie to
know how scared I was, so I helped him heave up
the heavy lid. It took all our strength, which is
perhaps why we paid no attention to Bertie's
barking.

"I can't look!" I said. "Is there a skeleton?"

Eddie gasped. "No!" He shone the torch and I
saw the light glittering on dull gold and silver and
catching the bright gleam of jewels.

Suddenly, another, stronger light shone down
on us.

"So, what are you two doing here?" asked
Sven. His powerful torch beam shone from the
trapdoor. He must have seen what was in the

tomb because he said, "I can see you've found something … the church treasures I've been looking for!"

"You won't get them!" I shouted, above Bertie's excited barking.

"This is our land!" Eddie called. "You can't take these away or we'll fetch the police."

"I think I'll just come and see for myself," Sven said in a creepy voice. He came down the first step.

I remembered Bertie liked games and Sven didn't like dogs. "Go for him, Bertie!" Bertie began to bark and growl even louder as he leaped up the stone steps.

Sven shot back. "Get him away!" he shouted. "I've got a knife outside! You wait!" He slammed the trapdoor shut.

"He's bluffing," I said, but my voice wobbled. "He'd never dare."

"These treasures must be worth a fortune. He might do anything to get his hands on them," Eddie said.

"We're trapped!" I found it hard to breathe.

"There might be a way out." Eddie shone his torch round the old stone walls. One part of the wall looked different. "It's a door!" he yelled.

If the wood hadn't been rotten we'd never have got it open. "We must take some of the treasures so he won't get them." I went back and pulled out a jewel-studded cup and a decorated cross, stuffing them in my backpack. The cross stuck out and kept banging the back of my head.

Eddie hesitated. "We don't know where the tunnel goes. And he might be bluffing and just run off."

"We don't have a choice! He'll come back, I'm sure. If he kills us and puts the trapdoor back, we might never be found."

Eddie thrust another jewelled cup into his backpack and we rushed through the door, with Bertie following. We tried to shut it but it sagged on its hinges. Sven wouldn't be held up for very long.

The tunnel reeked of damp and decay but Bertie thought it was a great adventure and ran ahead of us into the darkness.

"Could be a dead end," Eddie said, as we slithered and slipped over the wet stone floor.

Already I could hear a sound, echoing along the tunnel; a faint shouting as if Sven had come back into the room above.

The floor sloped steeply down now and I could hear Bertie scrabbling. Then I saw him by the light of my torch, digging away at a fall of earth and stones that blocked the end of the tunnel.

We could hear Sven scrambling and swearing and the sound was definitely coming nearer.

"How will we ever get out of this?" I asked despairingly.

9 Bertie the Hero

I reached into my pocket for my penknife with the idea we could use it to dig our way out. My fingers closed round the heavy Viking ring which was still in my pocket. A feeling of magic power flooded through me and I wished very hard on the ring to help us escape.

Suddenly I saw a sheen of moonlight coming through the hole Bertie was digging. "We can get out here!" I shouted.

We both scrabbled desperately beside Bertie with our bare hands, all the time hearing Sven's shouts getting nearer. The last bit of earth crumbled and we followed Bertie through into a cave, which was open to a beach at one end. We ran out to the beach. Cliffs reared above us.

"This is where my father was found," Eddie said. "This is the only beach on the island and you can only get here by sea. Dad rowed round here the day he died. We never came back for the boat."

Eddie ran to one side of the beach. "It's still there! Come on. We can't climb out of here to the causeway but we can go by boat."

We dragged the little rowing boat down the sand. "Get in and I'll push it off," Eddie was saying just as Sven came out of the cave, swearing and shouting. Bertie rushed at him, barking excitedly and Sven froze, giving Eddie time to push the boat into the water. I jumped in and Eddie followed.

I looked back, calling Bertie.
Moonlight gleamed on
something in
Sven's hand.
Then he
struck at
the dog.
There
was a
frightened
howl and
Bertie ran
to us,
limping. He
whimpered
as we hauled
him into the
boat and I felt
the wetness of
blood on my hand.

Eddie seized the oars and rowed wildly while I
tore my jumper off and pressed the pad against
the deep cut in Bertie's shoulder. When I looked
back, Sven had disappeared back into the cave.

"He'll try to get away over the causeway,"
Eddie said, rowing the boat round the little island,
making slow progress in the choppy sea.

I hugged Bertie as we were splashed by the waves, and I hated Sven with all my heart for hurting our dog.

When we rounded the island we saw the causeway was already under water. The dark figure of a man was struggling to walk along it. He was up to his knees in water and hampered by his backpack.

Eddie was rowing quite near him now. Suddenly Sven lost his footing and fell in. His head bobbed to the surface. "Help me!" he shouted. "I can't swim!"

"Serves you right!" I shouted back. "You wanted to kill us and you've hurt Bertie!"

We could see Sven was floundering as he tried
to scramble back to the causeway.

"He might drown," Eddie said.

"I suppose we ought to save him," I said
reluctantly, as Sven floated off the causeway,
calling desperately.

Eddie stopped rowing but then we saw the
waves had pushed Sven onto the tip of a small
rock, just below the island. "He's probably all
right now," Eddie said, and rowed like mad for
the shore.

The lights were on in the guest house and a
police car was outside when we staggered in,
carrying Bertie.

"How did you know?" I began, and then Mrs Cuthbertson hugged us both. She was crying. "I found you'd both gone! I was scared and rang the police."

Two police officers got up from the kitchen table. "I said they'd be back; up to some silly nonsense, I expect!" the older policeman exclaimed, frowning at us.

I plonked Bertie on the table, bleeding from his cut. "He's been knifed by Sven Larsen," I said, looking at their surprised faces.

Eddie joined in. "He wanted to kill us and steal the treasures hidden under the church on the island."

"Treasures! Sounds unlikely!" the policeman said, half smiling.

We undid our backpacks. Everyone stared as I brought out the jewelled cup and cross and Eddie pulled out an engraved silver cup.

"But please ring the vet first of all," I said urgently. Bertie's injury seemed much more important than catching Sven.

"So where is this man now?" one policeman asked.

"Hanging onto a rock near the island," Eddie said. "He can't swim."

The police rang the coastguard and went off to meet them and find Sven. Meanwhile, the vet arrived and gave Bertie an injection and stitched up the deep cut.

"Will he be all right?" I asked anxiously.

"Of course he will. Just keep him quiet for a few days," she said.

She didn't know Bertie!

* * * * *

Much later, when Mrs Cuthbertson was making tea and Bertie had eaten several biscuits, one of the police officers came back to say that they had picked up Sven and had taken him to the police station for questioning.

The police believed our story the next day when they found Sven's backpack washed up on the beach, containing candlesticks and another jewelled cross. They told us that Sven Larsen already had a police record. He had been an archaeology professor, but he'd found it more profitable to discover and steal ancient art treasures. He sold treasures through a dealer who then sold them abroad, where they couldn't be identified. The monks' book, which was very valuable, was found in Sven's car.

"And he seemed so nice," Mrs Cuthbertson said sadly.

The police said that all the church treasures would be taken to the museum after they had been valued. Mrs Cuthbertson was told that, as the owners of the island, she and Eddie would receive a big Treasure Trove reward.

"And all the treasures will stay here and be displayed in our local museum," Mrs Cuthbertson said. "Your father would be so pleased and proud of you."

"The money from the Treasure Trove will help us stay on in the house and mend the roof," Eddie said happily. Then he frowned. "I suppose there will be lots of archaeologists around but at least they won't be thieves!"

* * * * *

Mum and Dad brought Alice back from the hospital.

"What's the matter with Bertie?" Alice said, forgetting to hobble as she ran to him.

"I hope Sam's not been up to anything?" Dad asked anxiously.

Mrs Cuthbertson laughed. "Your Sam's a hero!" she said. "You won't believe it but Sven was a thief and an impostor. Eddie and Sam have been so clever and brave. They've found the church treasures hidden by the monks. They discovered an ancient and valuable book right under our house, and Sammy found a medallion from what sounds very like a Viking grave. I'm getting in touch with the archaeologists to come for another dig. Oh, and we'll be on TV after all!

I had a telephone call this morning from the local TV station!"

Alice stared at me, her mouth open. "Fancy Sammy being on TV!"

"You needn't sound so surprised!" I snapped. "And you've all forgotten Bertie. He found the Viking grave and he distracted Sven so we could get away." Then I remembered the bone Bertie found. "We found human bones under the house."

Mrs Cuthbertson went pale.

"In a secret cell next to our cellar, where I found the monks' book." Eddie said. "I suppose the police will have to make sure the skeleton is centuries old. We think he was a hermit, perhaps trapped in there."

We were all silent a moment.

Then I said again, "But Bertie's the hero, really."

Everyone patted him and Mrs Cuthbertson gave him a large bone – a beef one this time! He sprang out of his basket, immediately forgetting his wound, and hobbled out of the back door to find somewhere to bury it.

Eddie and I ran after him as he trotted to the dunes and dug a hole in the sand. I knew he'd be back the next day to dig the bone up. Then we walked slowly along the beach with him. Monks Island rose out of the mist just as it had when we arrived.

"It's weird to think about all that's happened in the last few days, isn't it?" I said.

"All those wonderful treasures hidden for so long, and Sven planning to do anything to get them, only to sell them abroad, so nobody here would ever see them."

"And what about the Vikings, forcing out and probably killing the monks to get at their gold and silver? And all for nothing, because it was hidden?"

"Perhaps it's better not to have any treasures,"
I said, fingering the Viking ring in my pocket.
Reluctantly, I gave it to him. "That will have to
go with the rest, I suppose." He'd

laugh at me but I had to tell him:
"I think those magic spells still
work, you know. I asked the
ring to get us out to safety."
Of course he did laugh. "Magic
runes and magic spells! Don't be
daft! It was luck – and Bertie."
He stroked the dog's head.

Bertie turned his head, whining. Loki was
sitting on a nearby dune. She was staring out at
the island, her tail twitching.

I had a feeling about
that cat. I was sure she
had lived many lives
before. Loki, spirit of the
Viking god, had seen
storms and calm,
blood and prayers, as
she returned to watch
over the treasures of
Monks Island.